*To Stephen
for the journey.*

SAB

*For my wife, Deborah,
and my daughters,
Allison and Caitlin.*

BF

When you hear the name *Mississippi River*,
what do you think of? A river as long as its name?

Some people think of locks and levees, dams and barges,
others of steamboats, paddle wheels, and showboats.
Some see cities and smokestacks lining its banks
or imagine rafting on it with Huckleberry Finn.
Some people call it the mighty Mississippi
and see it wide as a mile, and muddy.

But the mighty Mississippi isn't mighty when it begins.
It is a clear stream you can hop across on stones . . .

SPECIAL THANKS TO PAUL BENGSTON AND LARRY GARGUILLO.

BF

Library of Congress Cataloging-in-Publication Data

Baker, Sanna Anderson.
Mississippi going north / written by Sanna Baker ; illustrated by Bill Farnsworth.
p.   cm.
Summary: Describes the sights that can be seen canoeing north from the headwaters of the
Mississippi River through remote natural settings.
ISBN 0-8075-5164-3
1. Mississippi River—Description and travel—Juvenile literature. [1. Mississippi River—Description
and travel. 2. Natural history—Minnesota.] I. Farnsworth, Bill, ill. II. Title.
F351.B16 1996

917.7—dc20   95-52923
                                                                                                  CIP
                                                                                                  AC

THIS IS THE MOST
NORTHERN POINT
ON THE
MISSISSIPPI RIVER
TOWNSITE OF
MISSISSIPPI FORT

The design is by Karen A. Yops.
The illustration medium is oil on linen.
The text is set in Novarese Medium.

Mississippi Going North

Sanna Anderson Baker

Paintings by **Bill Farnsworth**

Albert Whitman & Company · Morton Grove, Illinois

The mighty Mississippi isn't mighty when it begins.
It is a clear stream you can hop across on stones.
It flows from a lake called Itasca, and a story says
it springs from the tears of an Ojibway maiden
made to dwell beneath the earth.

Ask most anybody, and they will say the Mississippi flows south.
But from its headwaters it sneaks north for miles
between walls of pine and birch.
Fallen trees make bridges from bank to bank.
You have to duck down in your canoe to pass under them.
Curtains of spiderwebs brush your face.

In places the river is paved with lily pads.
If you are very quiet, turtles sunning themselves might not plop
into the water when you pass.
If you let the current carry you, keep very still—
you may glide right by a great blue heron
watching for fish.

Around a bend, you may surprise a doe and her fawn
as they drink from the river.
In the woods, you might see a shadow and not know
if it's a grey wolf or a weathered tree.
One thing you will not see is people . . .

until you come to an old iron bridge.
There you can see children fishing.
As you glide below the bridge,
swallows swoop from their mud nests.
If you hoot,
your voice will echo.

Now the river flows into Bootleg Lake.
A red-winged blackbird perched on a reed doesn't stir
as you drift by. Out on the lake, a loon bobs on the chop.
If your paddle only whispers, you might get close enough
to see his red eye before he dives.

Suddenly he surfaces far away from your canoe.

Sun dances like angels on the water. A fish leaps.
It is not easy to spot the outlet where the river leaves the lake.
Finally you see it and paddle out
into a canyon of cattails.

It is shady and cool back on the river.
A breeze whistles in the tops of the pines.
Here and there beavers have gnawed trees.
If you are lucky, you will see a beaver or spy a dam.

After a day on the Mississippi going north,
food and rest sound good.
Up ahead a high sandbank plunges into the river.
You run your canoe aground and scramble up the bank.
A thick layer of pine needles cushions the earth,
soft for sleeping. Perhaps you wander into the woods
to look for kindling. Besides firewood you may find
wild aster and wintergreen.

If you coax a fire to life and cook your supper over it,
you can eat while you watch the sun set.

Finally, the sun and the fire die to embers, and night settles in.
Night sounds are loud. Was that an owl? Was that a wolf?
What creatures are out there awake in the night?

It is time to undo your bedroll on the carpet
of pine needles. Has a person ever slept in this spot before?
Perhaps a French explorer or an Ojibway hunter.

Suddenly waves the color of a luna moth's wings
wash across the sky.
Aurora borealis! Northern lights!

Aren't you glad there are still skies dark enough for seeing stars
and northern lights, still places where creatures' voices fill the night,
still wilderness where no roads go?

Aren't you glad you know
about the Mississippi going north?

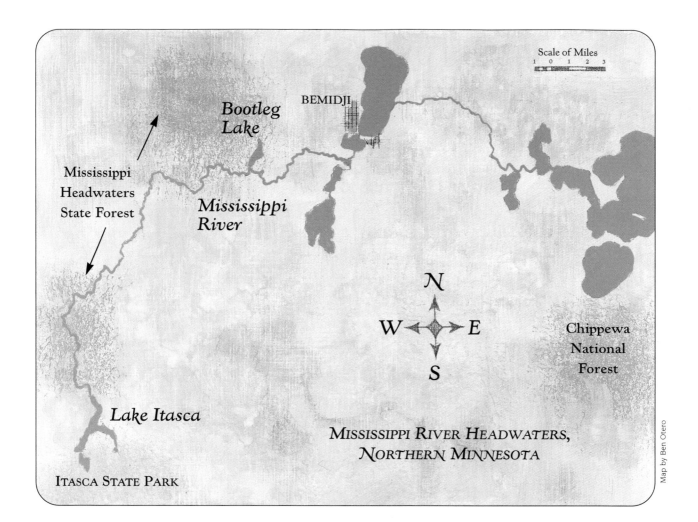

Scale of Miles
1 0   1   2   3

BEMIDJI

Bootleg Lake

Mississippi Headwaters State Forest

Mississippi River

N
W   E
S

Lake Itasca

ITASCA STATE PARK

Chippewa National Forest

MISSISSIPPI RIVER HEADWATERS, NORTHERN MINNESOTA

Map by Ben Otero

About 12,000 years ago, glaciers retreated from the region of the Mississippi headwaters. They left behind rolling plains and lake and river basins. It is thought that at this time the first people arrived. They were hunters who moved constantly in search of large prey such as woolly mammoths, mastodons, and giant ground sloths.

Eventually, the Dakota (Sioux) people claimed the area as their home. But in the early 1600s, the Ojibway (Chippewa) forced them out. For centuries, there was fighting between these groups over the territory. Europeans also came to what is now Minnesota during the 1600s. Explorers and trappers were among the first white people to see the headwaters of the Mississippi. In 1832 one explorer, Henry Schoolcraft, found the source of the great river, a lake which he named Itasca. Schoolcraft is also responsible for creating the "legend" of the Indian maiden whose tears are said to feed the waters of America's longest river.